WITHDRAWN

D0030059

Text copyright © 2015 by Anh Do
Illustrations copyright © 2015 by Jules Faber

ISBN 978-1-338-30565-4
10 9 8 7 6 5 4 3 2 1   19 20 21 22 23

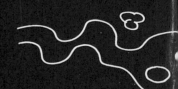

Printed in the U.S.A.   23
First U.S. printing 2019

Typeset in Chaloops Senior, Push Ups, and Lunch Box

BLAH, BLAH, BLAH

ANH DO

Illustrated by JULES FABER

WEiRDO 4

SUPER WEIRD!

SCHOLASTIC INC.

SUPER SAUSAGE

CHAPTER 1

You already know that me and my family are a **bit** weird!

weird
weird
weird
weird
weird
super weird
weird

also weird!

But guess what? Our new puppy, FiDo, is **WEIRD**, too!

1

FiDo's a sausage dog. He has **super-short legs** and a **super-looooooooong** body.

He can't jump very high, but he can **wriggle-under** almost anything!

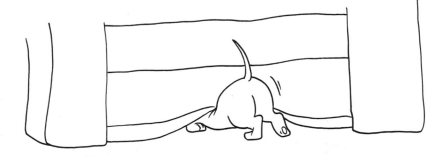

He keeps wriggling into **weird** places and finding things we haven't seen in **aaaaaaaaaaaages!**

Like Sally's **socks** . . .

**THAT'S WHERE
MY POLKA-DOT
SOCK WENT!**

And Dad's **gadgets** . . .

**YOU FOUND
MY OLD VIDEO
CAMERA!**

3

Roger's **pacifier** . . .

BINKY!

And Granddad's **teeth!**

MY OLD OLD TEETH!

4

FiDo's **really** brave. He's not scared of anything.

He's like a **SUPER** sausage dog.

IS IT A DOG? IS IT A SAUSAGE?
NO, IT'S **SUPER** SAUSAGE DOG!

Faster than a **speeding bullfrog!**

5

More **powerful** than a **crazy chicken!**

Able to get under **anything** in a single crawl!

6

In fact, both of our pets are **really brave**. Blockhead isn't scared of anything, either. He's like the **bravest parrot** in town!

He's so brave, they should name a **bravery award** after him.

OFFICER JACKSON, FOR BRAVELY RESCUING A FAMILY FROM THEIR SINKING BOAT, I AWARD YOU . . . A GOLDEN BLOCKHEAD!

7

Oh, I forgot . . .

Blockhead **IS** scared of one thing.

Just **one** thing.

Flashing lights!

EEEK!

8

But that's nothing, really.

Blockhead and FiDo have become **best friends**.

They **sing** together.

ZZz ZZZ

They **sleep** together.

They practice **barking** together.

WOOF!
WOOF!

WUFF!
WUFF!

10

HA HA HA

They even watch **funny** **TV shows** together.

Their **favorite** TV show is called **Funniest Pets**. People send in videos of their pets doing **funny things!**

HA HA HA

11

Blockhead and **FiDo** do <u>**tons**</u> of funny things, too. They like to run around together like this —

YEEHAH!

It's <u>**SO**</u> **funny** watching them **ride around** like that!

12

FiDo's not very fast, 'cause of his **little legs**.
But that's kind of why I like him **even more!**

I'm **short** and **can't run very fast**, either!

— Perfect! —

SUPER NOSE!

CHAPTER 2

I guess everyone has something they are good at (even me!). And my dad is **reeeeeally good** at **SMELLING** things.

It's like he's a **superhero**,

and **smelling things** is his **superpower!**

NOSEMAN to the rescue!

15

It would be **great** if he could
use his **power** to <u>fight crime</u>!

THANK YOU, **NOSEMAN!**
WITHOUT YOUR HELP, WE WOULD
NEVER HAVE <u>CAUGHT</u>
GARLIC-BREATH JONES!

16

If you talk to Dad for a bit, **he can tell what you ate** for breakfast!

GUESS WHAT I HAD FOR BREAKFAST?

OATMEAL AND A BANANA!

YES!

ME?

GREEN APPLE,
A TUB OF YOGURT . . .
AND A HANDFUL
OF DIRT!

WOW!

18

MEOW. MEOW. MOO?

BIRDSEED!

WOOF!

(I told you Blockhead was weird!)

19

He can even tell what **FiDo's** eaten!

WUFF!
WUFF!

HMM. HALF A CAN OF WOOFY YUM YUM. A BONE. A WORM . . . AND . . . MY SHOE! **FIDO!**

WUFF!
WUFF!

20

Dad says it's because he has

a GREAT nose.

He's **SO good** at smelling things that he can **smell smoke** from a **loooooooong** way away.

He's always ready to **leap** into action as soon as he smells smoke in the air. He's had a few **false alarms**, but he always says it's

better to be

safe than sorry . . .

Like, there was this one time when we were

hiking

with

Granddad . . . 》》》

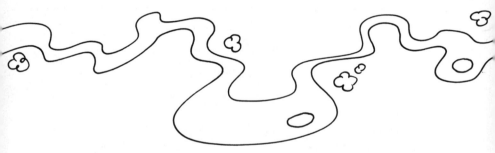

I SMELL SMOKE! I'LL SAVE YOU!

SPLAS

FIZZLE

FIZZLE

24

H!

OOPS, SORRY . . .

25

Then there was that other time when we were
at the retirement village

visiting

Great-Aunty Flo . . . 》》》》

WAIT!
I SMELL SMOKE!
I'LL SAVE YOU!

HAPPY BIRTHDAY TO YOU!

I AM OLD

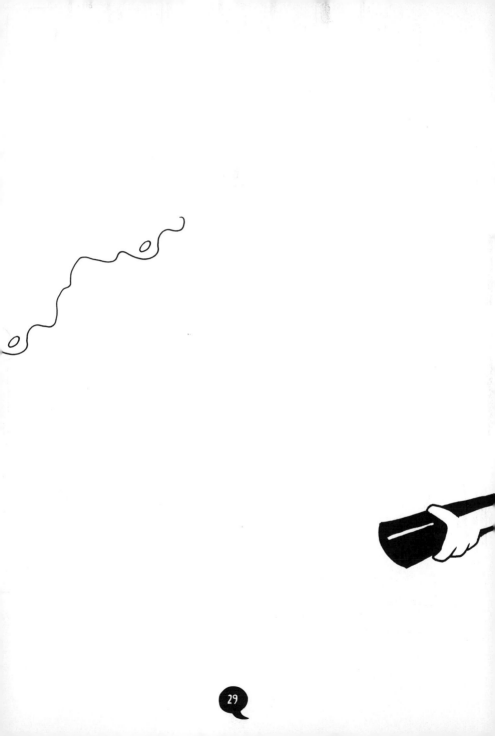

ZZZZHHHHHHHHHH

HTHHHHHHHH!

OOPS!

UM, HAPPY
BIRTHDAY!

31

But when there really is an emergency,
Dad and his **great nose** will make for one

AWESOME firefighter!

That's right, my dad's training to become
a FIREFIGHTER!

32

I've been going to training with him on the weekends. Just to watch. I think it would be a **very cool job**.

Maybe when I grow up and get a bit bigger, I can join him!

me, bigger!

We would make the **best** firefighting team!

33

But to become a firefighter, you have to reach a certain **height**. When they measured Dad, **he just made it!**

Lucky for Dad, he woke up that morning with **really bad bed head**. His **EXTRA-BIG** hair got him just over the line.

YOU MUST BE
THIS TALL

34

Bed head is really just another way of saying

WEIRD HAIR.

My whole family sometimes wakes up with **really funny** bed head.

Mom

Sally

35

Granddad

Me

But the **WORST** of all is Roger!

ROGER!

I often wish I were taller . . . 'cause being short can be **pretty annoying**.

Last year, our family went to the **carnival** and I was **too short** to go on the **big** roller coaster.

HEY, KIDS! YOU MUST BE THIS TALL TO RIDE!

37

They let kids **way younger** than me on
the ride, **just** because they were **taller**.

YAY!

BUT HE'S
JUST
A BABY!

How could they let a **giant baby** on
and not me? I think the rule should be:

**IF YOU'RE WEARING A DIAPER,
STICK TO THE KIDDIE RIDES!**

Believe me, **NO ONE** on a roller coaster
wants to sit next to someone who's able to

go to
 the bathroom
  in their own pants.

EWW

YAY!

EWWW!

39

And sometimes at the supermarket,
I can't reach my **favorite chips!**

They're <u>**always**</u> on the **top shelf!**

y

yuck

yuckier

yuc

worst chips,
yuck!

TOOTHPASTE
FLAVOR

CO
MED

BBQ | BACON & CHEESE | TOMATO | CHEESY CHEESE | CHICKEN

best chips, way up here

yum yum yum yum

uck yuck yuck yuck

yuckier yuckier me! way down here

GH INE | BRUSSELS SPROUTS | BURP FLAVOR

giant baby!

yuck

BBQ | BACON & CHEESE | TOMATO | CHEESY CHEESE | CHICKEN

best chips, still way up here

um | yum | yum | yum | yum

yuck | yuck | yuck | yuck

yuckier | yuckier | yuckier

me, still way down here

UGH ICINE | BRUSSELS SPROUTS | BURP FLAVOR

Maybe I should **JOIN THE CIRCUS** and learn to walk on stilts.

But I don't know if they'd allow that at the supermarket.

CAN THE KID ON THE STILTS PLEASE REPORT TO SECURITY **IMMEDIATELY?**

the best chips

But the **biggest problem** with being short
is that it makes it hard to play lots of **sports.**

Like basketball...

45

I wish there were a game called **SHORTBALL**.
It'd be **just** like basketball, but the ring would
be close to the ground.

All the **BIG GUYS** would **trip** over
themselves trying to shoot baskets and the

LITTLE GUYS
 would be the CHAMPS!

LITTLE
GUYS **00:00** TALL
GUYS

65

32

Who am I kidding?

Life is

p<u>rett</u>y tough

for **small guys!**

YEEHAH!

CHAPTER 3

Today, it's **PET DAY** at school! We all get to bring in our pets to show everyone.

It's **funny** how __so many__ people **look like their pets**.

Blake

Jake

49

Mullet

Ferret

Jenny

Penny

50

Mary

Scary

Toby Hogan

Hulk Hogan

51

But then there are others who look
nothing alike.

Like Henry . . .

and his dog

and his pet rock

Henry

Henry

Mo

Rocky

Then there's
Bella . . .

I thought Bella
would have
something like
a **fluffy** cat . . .

or a **long-eared bunny** . . .

or maybe a little **poodle** . . .

Man,
was I **wrong!**

53

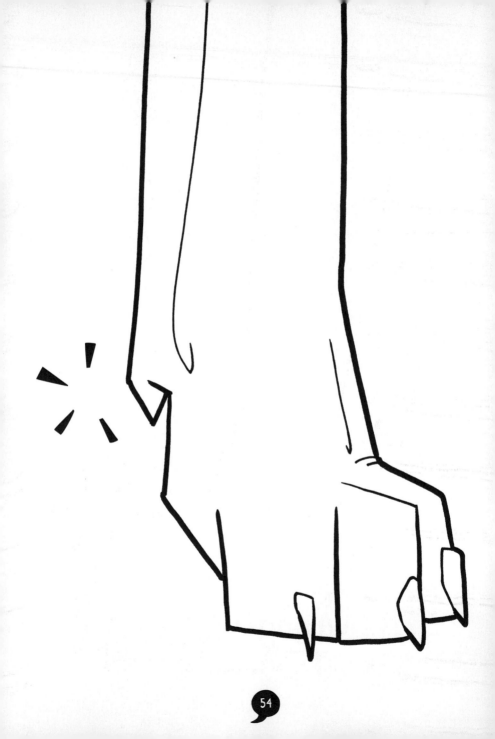

54

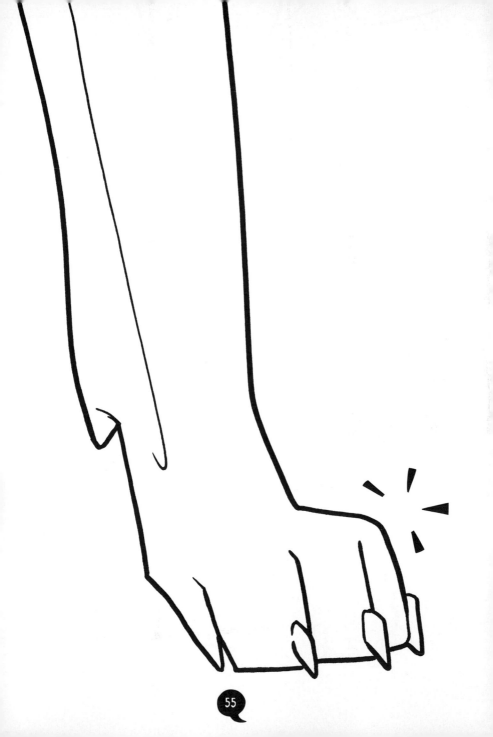

55

Bella has a **Great Dane** named Tiny!

WOW!

GASP!

WOW!

57

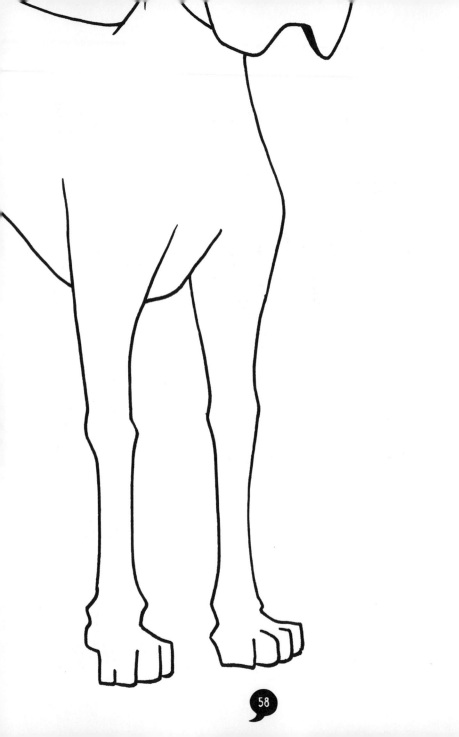

58

Tiny is **as big as a horse!**

A **really,**

really

BIG horse!

"Um, hi, Tiny," I said, walking up to him.

I'd never felt so small!

"He's friendly," said Bella. "Big, but friendly. Tiny," she said to the dog, "say hello to my friend WeirDo."

59

WOOO

His bark **nearly** blew me **over!**

WOW, BELLA, UMMM, CUTE DOG. IS HE GOING TO RACE IN THE KENTUCKY DERBY THIS YEAR?

Bella smiled at me, and I blushed.

"He likes you," said Bella. "I knew he would."

Then Tiny **licked** me!

62

SLURP!

63

I was knocked off my feet and landed with a

giant THUD!

HA HA HA HA HA

Bella helped me up.

SEE! HE REAAAAALLLY LIKES YOU!

That's funny, 'cause
I **reaaaaallly**
like Bella!

I showed Bella **my** pets.

"You must be FiDo," said Bella, "and you must be Blockhead."

She picked up FiDo and gave him a **cuddle**. Blockhead **jumped** onto her finger and **wriggled**.

HAHAHA!

Meanwhile, Mr. McDool was rounding up everyone and their pets for the

PET PARADE. >>>>

He'd even
brought in
his own pet!

The McDrools!

Everyone lined up with their pets and, **one by one**, we started making our way **around the playground**.

First, Tiny **galloped** along with Bella, and **everyone gasped**.

YIKES!

WHOA! GASP! YAY! GO, TINY!

Next, there were Wendy and her **rabbit** hopping backward,

a handstanding **pig**,

and a stunned **goldfish**.

70

Sally had given me her old **toy pony's saddle** to put on FiDo and a **cowboy hat** to put on Blockhead.

When they ran out with me—

Blockhead riding on the back of FiDo—

everyone laughed like

CRAZY!

And then to top it all off,
Blockhead **barked**!

WOOF
WOOF!

The crowd went **wild!**

After we'd run one lap,
the crowd asked for **MORE!**

MORE!

MORE!

MORE!

MORE!

72

So we ran around **again!**

And **again!**

WOOF WOOF!

Henry laughed **so much** that his juice

➤ **shot out his nose!**

73

FiDo and **Blockhead** were the

STARS

of the

SHOW!

"Quick," said Granddad. "Film them, Weir!"

I turned on the camera
just in time!

75

STAY TUNED!

CHAPTER 4

Everyone in our family loves hanging out with our pets.

Blockhead and Dad sometimes **dance together**.

electric boogaloo

77

Roger and Fido love **crawling** under **things** together.

Blockhead, Mom, and Sally sometimes have **sing-alongs**.

And I **really love** taking FiDo for **walks**.

CMON, FIDO, LET'S GO!

We like walking to the park near our house and playing a game where we **COPY each other**.

When Fido **rolls over**, I roll over.

When FiDo **pokes his <u>tongue</u> out**, I poke my tongue out.

When FiDo **lies back and sticks his legs in the air**, I lie back and stick my legs in the air.

Just then, I heard a voice . . .

HI, WEIR!
HI, FIDO!

It was **Bella!**

HI, BELLA

Bella was playing Frisbee with Tiny and asked if we wanted to join in.

Of course we did!

83

It was **SO MUCH FUN!**

We threw the **Frisbee**

all around

the park!

CATCH!

85

But then I threw the Frisbee <u>way</u> **too high** and it flew into a tree.

STUCK!

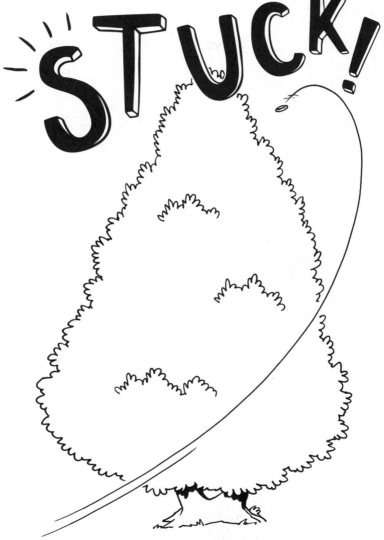

"Oops, sorry, Bella," I said. "You wait here. I'll climb up and get it."

So I **climbed** until I couldn't climb any farther and I reached as <u>**high**</u> as I could!

But I just

couldn't

reach it!

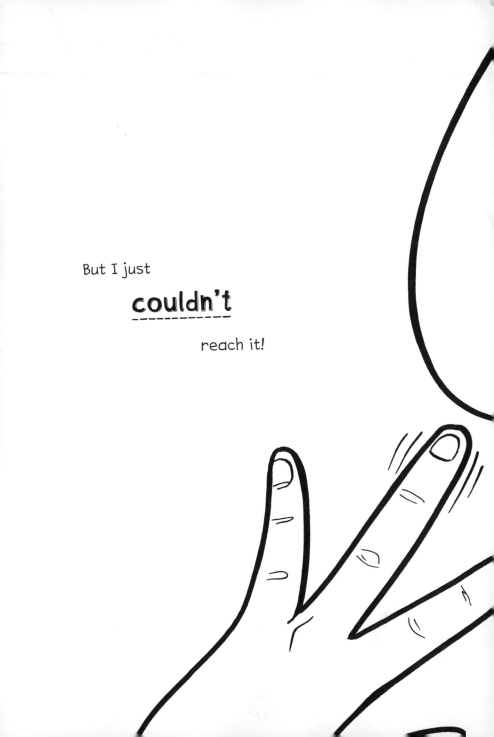

taller,

If only I were a **little bit** I would have been able to get the Frisbee back for Bella.

89

SORRY, BELLA

"That's okay, Weir," said Bella. "I'll go get my dad, and he'll be able to reach it."

I was **SOOO** embarrassed.

That night at dinner, I was telling Mom and Dad how **I wished I were taller**.

"That's all right," said Dad, "you're still growing."

90

"Yeah, but I'll never be **really** tall," I said.
"If I were taller, I'd be great at basketball."

COOL!

WOW!

"You might not be great at basketball, Weir,
but you're **really great at other things**,"
said Mom. "Like . . . **drawing!**"

It was true, I **could** draw.

91

A

B Fold line B over to meet line A

"Yeah," said Granddad. "And you're really good at **filming things**, too."

"That video you took of Blockhead and FiDo on Pet Day is **really cool**," said Sally. "Who knows, Weir, maybe one day you'll end up being a **famous movie director!**

Imagine that!"

YES, YOU'RE RIGHT. *TOY STORY 6* IS MY BEST MOVIE SO FAR.

WEIR DO

94

Just then, I came up with a **great idea!**

LET'S SEND THE VIDEO OF FIDO AND BLOCKHEAD TO *FUNNIEST PETS*!

How cool would it be if they were watching their **favorite TV show** together . . . and then saw themselves on it?!

YEAH! AWESOME! LET'S DO IT!

95

So Granddad and Sally helped me send in the video.

DONE!

We could **hardly wait** for the next episode of

Funniest Pets!

FiDo and Blockhead were **SOOO excited** to watch it, and they had **NO IDEA** that we'd sent **their video** to the show!

COMING UP NEXT, *FUNNIEST PETS!*

"Do you think they'll show the video of FiDo and Blockhead?" I asked Dad.

"Let's watch and find out!" said Dad.

As usual, the show was **HILARIOUS!**

There was a **piglet** in mud wearing rubber boots.

There was a **kitten** falling asleep on a piano . . .

and then

waking herself up
accidentally!

99

And a video of a **hamster** in a tiny hammock, wearing sunglasses.

But **no FiDo** and **no Blockhead** . . .

"Maybe they'll be on next week's show," said Sally.

"Yeah, maybe," I said.

All of a sudden, FiDo and Blockhead both started **barking!**

WUFF! WUFF!
WOOF! WOOF!

STAY TUNED, WE'VE SAVED THE BEST FOR LAST . . .

STAY TUNED!

HEY, COOL!

ONE OF OUR HOME VIEWERS—
A KID NAMED WEIRDO—
SENT US THIS AWESOME VIDEO
OF HIS PETS,
FIDO AND BLOCKHEAD!

We couldn't believe it! FiDo and Blockhead

WERE ON TV!

NUTS!

CHAPTER 5

In the morning, we woke to **LOUD** banging on the front door.

BANG! BANG!

BANG!

105

"Weir, could you please get it?" said Mom. "My hair looks **funny** again."

The banging on the front door kept going.

bed head

BANG!

BANG!

106

I climbed out of bed and wandered to the door.

I **couldn't believe** what I found there!

WEIRDO!

WEIRDO! OVER HERE!

WEIR! WEIRDO!

HUH?

WEIR, WEIR!

"What's going on?"
I asked Henry.

"The video!" he said.

108

"The video?"

"The video of FiDo and Blockhead on *Funniest Pets!*" said Henry. "The TV show! Everyone saw it! You're famous!"

★ FAMOUS? ★

WHERE'S FIDO? WHERE'S BLOCKHEAD? WE WANT TO SEE THEM!

109

"Uh, I don't know," I said. "I just woke up—"

"There they are!" everyone shouted.

Suddenly, **FiDo** poked his head out of the door and **Blockhead** landed on my shoulder.

110

The crowd went **nuts**, calling to them and rushing toward us to get a **better look**.

CAMERAS FLASHED.

111

And flashed.

And flashed.

112

There was a loud

SQUAWK!

beside me as Blockhead **panicked**.

Oh no.

"Please stop," I called out. "Blockhead doesn't like flashing lights!"

But it was **too late** . . .

BLOCKHEAD, WAIT!

114

He'd flown away into the sky, far, far away from the flashing cameras . . . and

far,

far

away

from home!

WUFF WUFF!

CHAPTER 6

We **searched** <u>**all day**</u> for Blockhead, but couldn't find him **anywhere!**

BLOCKHEAD!
BLOCKHEAD!
WHERE <u>ARE</u> YOU?

Henry and **Mo** joined in.

BLOCKHEAD,
BLOCKHEAD,
BLOCKHEAD!

WOOF?

Bella and **Tiny**, too.

AROOOOOO!

BLOCKHEAD!
BLOCKHEAD!

119

We looked in **all of his favorite places**.

We checked the **creek** where we sometimes take him for a bird bath.

BLOCKHEAD, WHERE ARE YOU?

BLOCKHEAD!

120

We checked the **bird shop** where we
buy his birdseed.

BLOCKIE?

PET
STORE

121

We even checked the **TV shop** where Blockhead and FiDo sometimes like to watch TV.

Sally and Henry helped me put up some
Missing posters.

LOST BIRD

Answers to Blockhead, Blockie, and Hey, Bird!

LIKES: Wriggling, mooing, barking. Most of all, likes playing with his best friend, FiDo.

DOESN'T LIKE: Flashing lights.

REWARD: Anything you like from Henry's pet rock collection.

I was **really worried** about Blockhead. I could tell FiDo was, too. He kept **wuff-wuffing**, calling out to his friend.

WUFF?
WUFF?

"It'll be okay," said Bella. "You'll find him."

"I hope so," I replied.

"Woof!" said Tiny.

Then he gave me and FiDo

a HUGE lick.

UMM, THANKS, TINY

We were all making our way back home when Dad got a phone call.

I got a **little bit** <u>**excited**</u>. Maybe someone had found Blockhead!

"It was the Fire Crew," said Dad. "Sounds like there might be a dog stuck in the old shed at school. They've asked me if I can go and check it out."

OH . . .

"Hey, Weir," said Dad, "why don't you and FiDo come with me?"

UMM . . .

"Come on," said Dad, "we'll keep a lookout for Blockhead on the way."

TO THE RESCUE!

It was **exciting** being on a **real-life**
firefighting job with Dad . . . except that

there was **no fire** . . .
and **Blockhead was still missing** . . .
and **I was at school** . . .

on the WEEKEND!

A few people were standing around, waiting for
us near the school gate.

"The barking was coming from over there," one lady said, pointing to the shed.

"Who knows how a dog got in there," said another guy, "but I'm sure he would like to get back out!"

"**Absolutely**," said Dad. "Come on, Weir and FiDo. **Let's go**."

WRIGGLE!

CHAPTER 7

Dad unbolted the shed, and we took a look inside.

We found a few **daddy longlegs** . . .

and even one
daddy short legs!

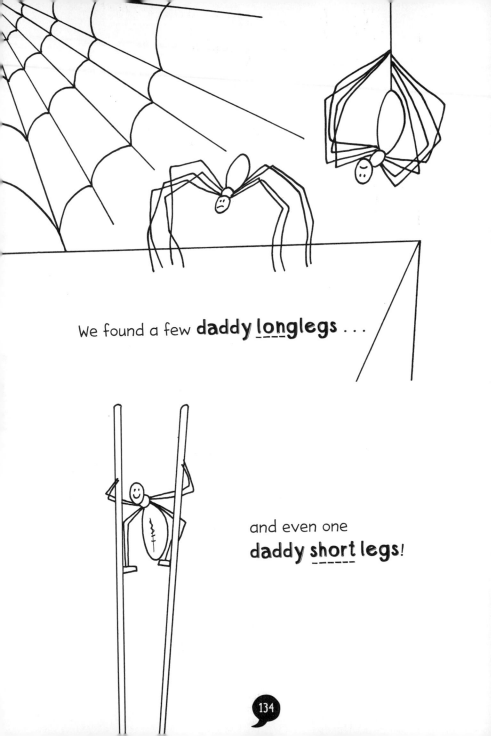

But there was **no sign of a dog**!

WHERE'S THE DOG?

NO IDEA . . .

WUFF?

We were thinking he must have found a
way out, when we heard **barking**!

WOOF!
WOOF! WOOF!

We looked inside again . . . but there was
definitely no dog in there!

136

Just the spiders!

NO DOG IN HERE!

NOPE!

HUH?

WHAT'S GOING ON?

STILL NO IDEA

WUFF!

137

WOOF WOOF

We'd just about **run out of ideas**, when we realized FiDo had wandered off.

We found him **wriggling** behind the back of the shed.

FiDo

138

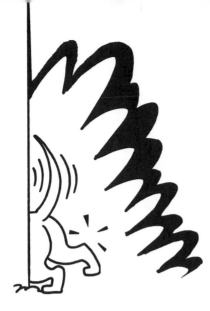

"FiDo, come back, boy," called Dad.

But FiDo **wriggled in farther**.

"FiDo," I called.

But he'd **already disappeared** behind the shed.

WUFF!
WUFF!
WUFF!

"What is it, FiDo?" I called out. "What have you found back there?"

Dad tried to follow him . . .

OOF!

He **tried** . . .

and **tried** . . .

UGH!

141

. . . and tried!

EEE!

But no amount of **wriggling** was going to
squeeze him through!

142

I suddenly realized that **I could fit** through!

"Dad, can I try?" I asked.

"Sure thing, Weir!"

Dad stepped out of the way, and I began **wriggling** behind the shed.

Wriggling behind the shed was **easy for me** . . . I guess

being small helps sometimes!

You **wouldn't believe** who I found back there!

TA-DA!

WOOF! WOOF! WUFF! WUFF!

144

There was no dog!

It was **Blockhead** who was **barking** all along!

YAY!

GO, WEIR!

145

TO THE RESCUE!

CHAPTER 8

Blockhead had hurt his wing flying behind the school shed, but he's **much better** already.

Everyone's been helping him rest up.

147

Especially FiDo and me.

149

Dad thinks I'll make an **awesome** firefighter one day. And maybe even FiDo could join me as a **rescue dog**.

TO THE RESCUE!

150

For Summer Do
the 4th
little Weirdo!

FROM ANH

DEDICATIONS

FROM JULES

For my mum and dad,
who encouraged me to be
anything I wanted,
as long as I gave it my best.

WEiRDO

ANH DO

Fitting in won't be easy... but it will be **FUNNY!**

Book 1

GOT IT!

Book 2

GOT IT!

WEiRDO 2 EVEN WEIRDER!

ANH DO